Dear Parent:
Your child's love of re

Every child learns to read in a diff
speed. Some go back and forth be
favorite books again and again. Otl
order. You can help your young reader improve and become more
confident by encouraging his or her own interests and abilities. From
books your child reads with you to the first books he or she reads
alone, there are I Can Read Books for every stage of reading:

SHARED READING
Basic language, word repetition, and whimsical illustrations,
ideal for sharing with your emergent reader

BEGINNING READING
Short sentences, familiar words, and simple concepts
for children eager to read on their own

READING WITH HELP
Engaging stories, longer sentences, and language play
for developing readers

READING ALONE
Complex plots, challenging vocabulary, and high-interest topics
for the independent reader

ADVANCED READING
Short paragraphs, chapters, and exciting themes
for the perfect bridge to chapter books

I Can Read Books have introduced children to the joy of reading
since 1957. Featuring award-winning authors and illustrators and a
fabulous cast of beloved characters, I Can Read Books set the
standard for beginning readers.

A lifetime of discovery begins with the magical words "I Can Read!"

Visit www.icanread.com for information
on enriching your child's reading experience.

For Bonnie

HarperCollins®, 🐾®, and I Can Read Book® are trademarks of HarperCollins Publishers Inc.

Library of Congress Cataloging-in-Publication Data

Hoff, Syd, date
   Happy birthday, Danny and the dinosaur! / story and pictures by Syd Hoff.
      p.   cm.—(An I can read book)
   Summary: Six-year-old Danny invites his dinosaur friend to come to his birthday party.
   ISBN-10: 0-06-026437-3 (trade bdg.) — ISBN-13: 978-0-06-026437-6 (trade bdg.)
   ISBN-10: 0-06-026438-1 (lib. bdg.) — ISBN-13: 978-0-06-026438-3 (lib. bdg.)
   ISBN-10: 0-06-444237-3 (pbk.) — ISBN-13: 978-0-06-444237-4 (pbk.)
   [1. Dinosaurs—Fiction. 2. Birthdays—Fiction.] I. Title. II. Series.
PZ7.H672Had 1995
[E]—dc20
                                                                         95-2710
                                                                            CIP
                                                                             AC

❖

I Can Read!™

BEGINNING 1 READING

Happy Birthday, DANNY and the DINOSAUR!

Story and Pictures by

SYD HOFF

HarperCollins*Publishers*

Danny was in a hurry.

He had to see his friend

the dinosaur.

"I'm six years old today,"
said Danny.
"Will you come
to my birthday party?"

"I would be delighted,"
said the dinosaur.

Danny rode the dinosaur

out of the museum.

On the way

they picked up Danny's friends.

"Today I'm a hundred million years

and one day old," said the dinosaur.

"Then it can be your party too!"
said Danny.

The children helped Danny's father

hang up balloons.

"See, I can help too,"
said the dinosaur.

13

Danny's mother gave out party hats.

"How do I look?"

asked the dinosaur.

"We would like to sing a song,"
said a girl and a boy.

They sang,

and everybody clapped their hands.

"I can sing too," said the dinosaur.

He sang,

and everybody covered their ears.

"Let's play pin the tail

on the donkey," said Danny.

The dinosaur pinned the tail

on himself!

The children sat down to rest.
"Please don't put your feet
on the furniture," said Danny.

The dinosaur put his feet
out the window.

Danny's mother and father

gave each child

a dish of ice cream.

They had to give the dinosaur
more!

"Here comes the birthday cake!"
said the children.

They counted the candles.

"One, two, three, four, five, six."

The dinosaur started to eat
the cake.

"Wait!" said Danny.

"First we have to make a wish!"

"I wish we can all be together again next year," said Danny.

"I wish the same thing," said the dinosaur.

They blew out the candles.
"Happy birthday to you!"
everybody sang.

"This is the best birthday party
I have ever had," said Danny.
"Me too," said the dinosaur.